MRS. R. SNUGGLESWORTH

Mrs. R. Snugglesworth,
Attorney-at-Law

By: Amy Flanagan (Batavia, IL), Illustration: Jon Davis

MRS. R. SNUGGLESWORTH

ATTORNEY-AT-LAW

AMY FLANAGAN

For Gene, Chase, Riley, and Tenzing

Mrs. R. Snugglesworth

Maple Lane

Dr. P.

Dr. Shadow

Austin

Howard

Big Ten

Brooks

Popsicle

Pitter Patter

Torts

Teapot

Clarinet

Hurricane

Ozzie

Hiccup

PROLOGUE

For the first few years of my life, I did the usual dog things—snacks, long naps, fetching, power naps—as well as developing some special talents: I look great in a bandana. I am top-notch at drinking out of mud puddles, and I run through the sprinkler like it's my job. If there was a Dog Running Through the Sprinkler event at the Olympics, not a soul could compete. I am that good. Honestly though, I was getting a tiny bit bored. I needed something new in my life. Perhaps something that would exercise my mind. But what could that be? Crossword-puzzle champion? World-class chef? Builder of custom furniture? Philosopher? Electrician? Best-selling author? Ski instructor?

I found the solution to my boredom where I least expected it—during one of my regular, same-old, same-old visits to our local Bark Park.

Jury duty.

I didn't plan for it to happen. It was the first time I'd ever been on a jury. Now, you might be wondering if canine jury duty is anything like what you see on those shows your tall humans watch on TV. Kind of, only *way* more interesting, and no one is wearing an uncomfortable suit. When a dog is accused of breaking one of our Dog Laws, they usually get a lawyer to help them get out of trouble. Their case is heard in court at the Bark Park, in front of a judge and a jury. The judge makes sure that the dog lawyers follow

1

the rules of the court. The jury listens to the facts that the lawyers present and, based on those facts, they decide whether the accused dog is guilty or innocent of breaking the law. And we wear whatever we want, which is usually just a snazzy collar.

Jury duty in my world is mostly an accidental affair. Your person takes you to the local Bark Park, throws a tennis ball, and the next thing you know, you've careened yourself right into the judicial system. Some dogs think jury duty is a real drag and will do anything to get out of it—fake a broken toe, pretend something's in their eye, or claim they have a "bathroom emergency." That's the biggest lie of all. When the whole world is a bathroom, it's never an emergency.

For me though, being on that jury felt like something special—like the day I found that slightly used grilled cheese sandwich waiting for me on the sidewalk, at the very moment I was craving a snack. I am the Best at Finding Slightly Used Sandwiches.

I tipped my head to the side during that first day of jury duty, listening carefully as each side presented their arguments. I tried to consider only the facts, and tried even harder to ignore the antics of the other jurors.

The lawyers completed their arguments. The judge stared straight at us: "Jurors, you have an important task ahead of you. You must rely on the facts to decide on the guilt or innocence of the accused and set your feelings aside. Now go."

After we delivered our verdict, the judge pulled me aside. "I could tell you put some real thought into what you heard today. Have you ever considered law school?" she asked.

I immediately set aside all thoughts of becoming a Ski Instructor-Electrician-Crossword-Puzzle Champion and applied to Wagsworth Legal Academy, the Bark Park's *best* canine law school.

CHAPTER ONE

My name is Mrs. R. Snugglesworth, Attorney-at-Law. At four barks long, it's a mouthful. I usually go by Mrs. R. I'm a butter-colored English Labrador Retriever. Picture your standard tallish American Labrador Retriever, make her six inches shorter and add an extra bundle of snuggly chins. If that's too hard to imagine, just imagine seventy-pounds-of-low-to-the-ground PRECIOUS. I am the Best at Being Precious. And I was also going to be the Best at Law School.

The first day of law school arrived quickly. I thought I'd never get my family out the door. Unfortunately, I cannot drive, and the Bark Park is a bit of a hike from our home. We go to the Bark Park every day, so you'd think they'd have their routine figured out by now. Eventually, we piled into the minivan and made the three-mile drive to the Bark Park.

A quick word about my family. Two of my family members are especially cool. Their human names are... hmmm. Something. I forget. In my head, I call them Snickerdoodle Fuzzlebean (Snicker, for short), and Crunchy Potato Chip (Crunchy, for short). Snicker is eleven and Crunchy is eight. The other two? They are grown-ups. Snicker and Crunchy call them Mom and Dad, but in my head I call them The Kitchen and The Vacuum. I usually stick to dog food but occasionally The Kitchen drops something irresistible onto the tile, like a ham. A beautiful ham. I am the Best at Loving Ham, especially if it falls on the floor, which is where ham goes to soak up extra flavor. One time she dropped an Entire Ham... and you KNOW that I was on it in a flash! I dragged that treasure straight into the yard, for safety reasons that I cannot explain to you right now. I will say that on this occasion I realized that The Kitchen does not approve of Yard Ham. But then again, she never has understood fine dining.

And then there's The Vacuum. I am not sure if he was born with the vacuum attachment or what. Either way, he is CONSTANTLY using it and messing up my decorating ideas that I bring to life through careful and strategic shedding. Each hair I shed is intentionally placed in just the right spot. (And yes, sometimes that spot is on the couch, an area of the house from which I am unfairly excluded.) Then he comes along a few times a week and vacuums it right up!

I don't mean to complain about The Vacuum and The Kitchen. Rumor is they are the reason our family has things like food and a house. I constantly overhear conversations at the dinner table where The Vacuum says something like, "When you have a job, you can buy your own house and add a waterslide to your bedroom". I presume he's speaking to Snicker and Crunchy because A) I am working towards a law degree, and B) I would never install a waterslide. I would install a boss sprinkler system with a snack bar. Obviously.

We parked at the Bark Park and Snicker grabbed my leash as I exited the minivan. We walked past the soccer fields and the portable toilets. Talk about information overload. So many smells! Usually, I like to take a quick detour in that direction, but I didn't want to be late for my first day of class.

We walked on, past the pond where I do my very best swimming. I adore swimming. My paws are extra-big which means I am the Best Swimmer. I am also the Best at Leaving the Most Tennis Balls in the Pond—probably because it's one of my main hobbies.

We continued through the field and finally reached the gate. Crunchy lifted the latch and we entered the Bark Park. My tail wagged like high-speed windshield wipers. Sure, I go to the Bark Park every day, but... you know how it is on the first day of school.

Wagsworth Legal Academy holds classes in a special fenced-off area of the Bark Park. If you saw it, you'd probably think it was just a field with a few pieces of unusual-looking playground equipment. You might even think it was an agility course, like the kind they have in fancy dog shows on TV. (I am the Best at Napping when those shows are on. I don't want anyone to get any ideas. There's way too much bathing in that line of work.)

After Crunchy took off my leash, I took a deep breath and ran over to the Academy for a little meet-and-greet with my fellow students.

"Hey! Hey! Hey!" I heard what appeared to be a *very* high-energy terrier. He bounded right over to me. I responded with what I hoped was a lawyerly bark and introduced myself.

"I'm Mrs. R. Snugglesworth. I'm new and I am so happy to be here and—"

"That's nice. Really. I'm happy that you're happy. My name is Maple Lane. You've probably heard of me."

"No, I'm sorry, can't say that I have. Do you live near—"

"Well listen," he interrupted, "I'm going to be the Best Lawyer that Wagsworth Legal Academy's ever seen. And you know what? You look more like a furry rhinoceros than a dog. Are you sure you're at the right place?"

I looked right at him. "Personally, I think a furry rhinoceros sounds delightful—like a snuggly freight train."

"Whatever," he said.

I am the Best at Snappy Comebacks. Furthermore… HOLD ON A MINUTE. Did Maple Lane just say he was going to be the Best Lawyer? With a capital "B"? Surely, I misheard him. After all, *I* am going to be the Best Lawyer. It *was* hard to focus with him bouncing all over like a kangaroo. Even my Top-Notch Expert Hearing fails now and again.

Out of the corner of my eye, I saw that the Legal Beagles had arrived. I zoomed past Maple Lane. Class was about to start.

Wagsworth Legal Academy is just like any highly regarded law school, with a few small differences.

1. All of the classes are outside.
2. It only takes seven days. (Hey! We only live for ten to fifteen awesomely fun-packed years. We can't spend three years in law school like humans do.)
3. Also, all of the students and professors are dogs. (All of the classes are usually taught by a Beagle who is at the very top of their field. Beagles are known for teaching law school because their name rhymes with "legal." It's in their DNA. Everyone knows this.)

I arrived at the classroom and exchanged get-to-know-you sniffs with my fellow students. My class contained eight dogs of different shapes, sizes, and personalities. One of the Legal Beagles barked sharply, and we settled down to listen.

"Greetings, new students! My name is Geraldine Prudence. You can call me Dr. P. Over there, you see two of the other professors: Teapot and Torts. Today you begin your study of canine law. These laws are the rules that we all follow to enjoy happy dog lives. The classwork at Wagsworth Legal Academy is divided into two sections: Case Law, and Stealth Evidence Gathering and Forensics. Together, we will focus on the case law of the three most important cases of our time: The Case of the Mis-STEAK-en Identity, the Case of the Misguided Photo Bomb, and finally, the Case of the Killer Paw. All of our laws are built on these cases."

I gave a sharp bark of acknowledgment. These cases were huge! They were in all the big peemails. I am the Best at Reading Big Peemails. Actually, I am the Best at Reading the *headlines* of all the Big Peemails. The Kitchen likes to rush me along when I am reading and sometimes I have to skip over the details.

A quick word on peemails. They are kind of a huge deal. It's how we communicate with one another—and unlike humans, we read with our noses instead of our eyes! Isn't that neat? Very cheap and guess what else? Dogs can read peemails in any language!

"As dogs, we don't live nearly as long as humans, although we squeeze a lot of life into those years," Dr. P. said. "Because of that, Wagsworth Legal Academy goes much faster than human law school. As I am sure you are all aware, dogs are significantly smarter than humans and we learn much faster than they do."

We nodded. Humbly, of course.

Dr. P. continued. "In addition, I am very happy to announce that we have hired a new professor, Dr. Shadow, to teach our second section: Stealth Evidence Gathering and Forensics. Dr. Shadow is a mini goldendoodle known for his brilliance in teaching invisibility, which is one of the main skills a lawyer needs when collecting evidence. Not only is Dr. Shadow an expert in invisibility, he is also an expert in wearing adorable outfits *and* medicine. For example, he recently went to a barbecue where he became so concerned about one guest's unhealthy diet that he snatched the steak right off his plate, *while* wearing a brand-new plaid bow-tie."

I nodded. That's the mark of an excellent physician. Perhaps I'd ask Dr. Shadow for advice about my allergies. I am very sneezy.

"Now students—we have divided you into four groups of two. Each group will have a chance to learn from each of the four professors—myself, Teapot, Torts, and Dr. Shadow. To receive your degree and proudly add 'Attorney-at-Law' to the end of your name, you must do *either* of these things: 1) Prove your knowledge of all three examples of case law and invisibility or 2) Prove your invisibility skills AND pass one more test. Or, should I say, you must jump over THE BAR." This bar is another way in which Wagsworth Legal Academy is just like human law school. To become a human lawyer, you have to "pass the bar". I guess they jump over it although I've never seen this happen, even on TV. I bet it takes them A LOT of tries. Naturally, we canine lawyers have our own bar.

My ears flattened with worry as I gazed across Wagsworth Legal Academy and looked at the bar. I'll be honest. As seventy-pounds-of-low-to-the-ground PRECIOUS, I was certain to be stunningly good at going A) Under the bar, and B) Around the bar. But over the bar? I was going to pay strict attention in every class and go for option 1—that way I wouldn't have to think about the bar.

I put those thoughts aside to listen. Dr. P. was assigning us to our groups. I sat patiently, waiting to hear my name. It was starting to feel like I'd never get my assignment when Dr. P. finally said, "Let's see... that leaves... Mrs. R. Snugglesworth and Maple Lane! You'll be with Dr. Shadow."

I did a teeny-tiny groan inside my head. I *really* did not want to be partners with Maple Lane. The ego on that dog! And I was fairly certain that he didn't want to be partners with me. Still, I am the Best at Rising to the Occasion. I would work with Maple Lane.

My fur ruffled in the breeze as Maple Lane dashed past me to get to Dr. Shadow. I caught up to them just in time to hear Maple Lane say, "You know, Dr. Shadow, I wouldn't be surprised if I teach YOU a thing or two about stealth investigative techniques. I'll take it slow though, so Mrs. ARGHHH can keep up."

"It's Mrs. R.!" I barked.

Maple Lane was going to test my patience.

"Dr. Shadow, a pleasure to meet you," I interjected. "I'm Mrs. R. Snugglesworth, but you can call me Mrs. R. I'm eager to learn from you."

"A warm welcome to both of you," barked Dr. Shadow. "Let's get right to work. Today's lesson will focus on the most important evidence-gathering technique that exists: Invisibility."

I nodded. Of course! For a dog that masters invisibility, the rewards are breathtakingly comfortable. Invisible dogs can lay on any couch, any bed, any pile of coats at a party that they want, even if they've been told not to. They simply blend in! The trick is to stay very, very still and ignore any activity around you, until your human acknowledges your stealth genius. And whatever you do, DO NOT make eye contact! Usually they say something like, "Look who thinks they're invisible!" I confess that I could use some work in this area. I rarely hear, "You're so good at being invisible!" Usually I hear something like, "Mrs. R.! You know you're not supposed to be on the couch. Get down!"

I settled onto the ground to listen. Not only would Dr. Shadow teach me invisibility tactics that would help me gather evidence, I'd also learn how to stay invisible when I am trying to take a power nap on the couch.

"To be truly invisible," continued Dr. Shadow, "You must possess the stillness of an empty food bowl. Slow your breathing and close your eyes with the gentle grace of a spoon scooping into a fresh jar of peanut butter. Remain still when a human enters the room. Do *not* look their way. If you cannot see them, they *cannot* see you. You will know you've achieved invisibility when you hear your human say something like, 'You're so good at being invisible!' and then they walk away. This, my students, is a measure of your success. When you've mastered this skill, you can investigate from anywhere, including couches and beds that you aren't usually allowed to sit on."

Maple Lane said, "I already know how to do this. Watch me!" He jumped onto a nearby bench.

Right away, his person joined him on the bench and remarked, "Maple Lane! You're disappearing before my eyes. You are so good at being invisible!" He patted Maple Lane on the head and walked away.

Maple Lane jumped down from the bench and triumphantly trotted over to where Dr. Shadow and I were waiting.

"Well done, Maple Lane!" barked Dr. Shadow. "That was an excellent example of invisibility."

"Thank you, Dr. Shadow. I am the Best at Being Invisible," he replied.

Best at Being Invisible? Excellent example? What? That was pure luck! He didn't even have to try!

Dr. Shadow interrupted my thoughts. "Mrs. R., would you like to try?"

"Of course!" I barked confidently. Truthfully, I was a smidge nervous.

I ran to the bench and leapt up. I lowered myself onto the seat, starting with my front paws and gently settling my back half. A light breeze tickled my nose. I pictured my food bowl—empty, silver—and closed my eyes. My eyelids settled into place so smoothly I wasn't just the spoon in the peanut butter jar—I was the peanut butter. I snored a tiny, delicate fake snore.

Dr. Shadow whispered, "Oh my. That's a very advanced move. She's a natural."

With my eyes still firmly closed, I smelled Crunchy (crackers and couch cushions) and The Kitchen (olive oil) approaching the bench. Would they say the words I longed to hear—"Mrs. R., you are the Best at Being Invisible!"— and then depart?

I lay like a stone as they stood behind the bench talking. So far, so good. I resisted the urge to look at them. I am a True Professional.

I heard Crunchy chattering away. "What's for dinner tonight? Can we have burgers?"

"YES!" I thought to myself. I adore burgers. All that beef! I usually park myself right next to the grill. Being the Best Grill Supervisor is a natural extension of my Best Kitchen Supervisor skills.

Everything was going my way. There I was, my first day of law school, showing remarkable success at invisibility practice, AND we were having burgers for dinner. What a day! I just needed Crunchy or The Kitchen to comment on my invisibility, and then stroll away. What was taking so long? I snored another tiny, precious snore.

"Sounds good. I'll take some veggie burgers out of the freezer," replied The Kitchen.

Veggie burgers? WHAT? WHY? I tried not to gag. Now, I have enjoyed many a delicious veggie burger—chickpeas, quinoa, maybe a sensation of carrot… with… dare I say it…

a whisper of pumpkin? But I am here to tell you that they are not what The Kitchen does best. Her recipe is gross. GROSS. Seriously. It's been in all the Big Peemails (written by Yours Truly).

"Be cool," I told myself. "Do not panic. Stillness. Empty bowls. Peanut butter."

My breathing slowed as thoughts of peanut butter took hold. Things were back on track. A breeze floofed the fur around my generous eyebrows and tickled my nose. No. NO. Oh no. It can't be. Within that innocent gust lurked one of my greatest enemies—pollen.

I sneezed.

Crunchy leaned over the bench. "MRS. R., my little Twisty Sprinkle-Star, are you okay? Are your allergies bothering you?"

My allergies are legendary at the vet's office. I don't like to brag. BUT. I am highly allergic to thirteen different grasses, eighteen types of weeds, thirty-one trees, five mites, and two types of fungi. The vet said he'd never seen anything like it. Every six weeks I pop into the vet's office for an allergy shot. They love me there.

Meanwhile, Maple Lane was laughing. "Nice work, *Mrs. Sneezeworth*!"

I jumped down from the bench and trudged back to where Maple Lane and Dr. Shadow were waiting.

"Mrs. R., that was an excellent effort, but your unfortunately timed sneeze revealed your presence to your humans," said Dr. Shadow.

"Yeah," said Maple Lane. "You were terrible!"

"Maple Lane! Please provide constructive feedback only,"

barked Dr. Shadow. "You may've successfully made yourself invisible, but you didn't have nearly the challenge that Mrs. R. had. Maintaining invisibility while a discussion about veggie burgers occurs nearby is almost impossible. I would struggle to do it myself. And then to make it through that challenge only to give herself away with a sneeze? Mrs. R., I know you must be disappointed. I encourage you to practice at home. Don't give up. You can try again at our next class."

"Thank you, Dr. Shadow," I replied.

I heard Snicker calling for me. It was time to go home. As I turned to leave, Maple Lane barked, "You better practice a LOT, *Mrs. Strugglesworth!*"

I turned back to Maple Lane and did something I never usually do. I growled.

CHAPTER TWO

We spent the rest of the morning at home. It had turned into a beautiful day. After lunch, The Kitchen asked, "Who's ready for a walk?"

I responded with my Best Tail Wagging. I love walks.

We popped out the front door, down the steps, and made our way to the end of the driveway. I sat down and waited.

"Let's go!" commanded The Kitchen.

When it's just me and The Kitchen or me and The Vacuum, I walk on their left. If there's more than one human, I always walk between them, and just a tiny bit in front, because I am the Best Line Leader. Also, I do my

Best Thinking when I'm the Line Leader, and I had some serious thinking to do.

As The Kitchen and I walked, I thought about Maple Lane. He thought that he would upset me by calling me a Furry Rhinoceros and Mrs. ARGHHH. Please. I *am* delightfully fuzzy *and* very strong. My running is as strong and stylish as the finest rhinoceros! And you know what? He can laugh at me all he wants. Mrs. R. doesn't give up that easily! But then, he did call me Mrs. *Sneezeworth*. And Mrs. *Strugglesworth*. He forgot the "R" twice! I bet he did that on purpose.

I confess, that got to me.

What is up with this Maple Syrup character? Wait. That's not right—it's Maple LANE. Or should I say, Maple *Leaf*? Oh, that is a good one! Then a tiny wave of shame came over me, and I slowed down, nearly stopping on the sidewalk. What was happening to me? Name-calling? Growling? If the first day of law school was having this effect on me, what would I be like by the end of the week?

I paused at the oak tree a block from our house to read the latest peemails while The Kitchen tapped her foot impatiently. I find this behavior somewhat irritating. I have never interrupted her when she's trying to read *her* news. Okay, so I might interrupt her occasionally, but that's only because I have something important to bring to her attention—like when my surveillance reveals that another dog is walking down the sidewalk in front of our house. Trespassers! You'd think she'd thank me for alerting her.

I had lots of messages to catch up on, so she was just going to have to wait. Ozzie, who looked like a furry bouncy ball, had a new, loud, demanding, stinky housemate that was his size and took up a ton of time. Whatever it was, it sounded gross, except for the smelly part. That sounded amazing.

There was a long note from my friend Popsicle. Popsicle was a lovely mix-up of many ancestors and lived with his family near the elementary school. According to his peemail, he'd recently eaten a weeks-old peanut-butter-and-jelly sandwich that he found in the bushes. It did not end well. Poor Popsicle. Once I ate a not-so-gently-used cinnamon roll I found on the sidewalk. That didn't end well either.

Suddenly, I paused. My nose caught something… different mixed in among all the usual news. Nerves. Worry. Injustice. Something that wasn't right. The odor of unfairness overpowered the name of the dog who left the message. I pressed my nose to the ground and sniffed harder, trying to figure out the author of the peemail. Grass poked into my nose. Still, nothing. Frustrated, I raised my head and wandered in a slow circle, thinking.

This scent reminded me of the time I was falsely accused of stealing Crunchy's blue socks. Was I typically guilty of this offense? Of course! I am the Best at Top Secret Sock Collecting! I love socks. They are almost as fun as a tennis ball! But that time I really WAS innocent (blue is not my best color), and I got in trouble anyway! I could've really used a lawyer to help me out of that mess, but… the thing is, at the time of the Great Sock Debacle we were in the middle of a deep freeze. I'm not a big fan of being outside in those conditions. My tootsies are quite delicate. I mean really, would YOU go outside in bare feet during a deep freeze to drop off a peemail? In the end, I managed the situation without a lawyer but it would've been way easier with one by my side.

But this dog? This dog DEFINITELY needed a lawyer! Now, technically, I wasn't a lawyer yet, but I was *in law school*, which is the practically the same as *being* a lawyer. If I took the case, surely I'd have my degree by the time our court date arrived. I left a peemail, offering my legal services. I hoped that this troubled soul would contact me soon.

CHAPTER THREE

That evening, Snicker took me for a short walk before bedtime. Based on my careful observations, I have determined that he is allergic to wearing pants and weather-appropriate shoes. Even in winter, he wants to wear shorts and flip-flops! And a hat? Or gloves? Forget it. I worry that someday we will find him frozen to the back porch and I will be called upon to lick him until the ice melts from his flip-flops and he can get back inside.

We set off and I hustled back to the oak tree. I wanted to catch up on the news of the day. I crossed my paws for good luck, hoping that there'd be a response from the Falsely

Accused, a.k.a. my first potential client. I put my super-sniffer near the base of the tree and practiced sniffing my most Attorney-at-Law sniff. And there it was! Mixed in with an update on Popsicle's PB & J disaster and a greeting from Bernadette, our new greyhound neighbor, was a peemail from my new client. I sniffed carefully, soaking up the details of the case. My gosh, the Falsely Accused was my extra-tall friend Pitter-Patter! Pitter-Patter is a Great Dane.

"Time to go, Mrs. R.!" said Snicker.

I ignored him and kept sniffing. I had to know more. The more I sniffed, the more alarmed I became.

A few days ago, Pitter-Patter had found a tiny, muddy, stuffed bunny named Hiccup in his backyard. He knew Hiccup was important, so he brought his discovery to his human, Mr. Garcia. To Pitter-Patter's surprise, Mr. Garcia

was quite upset with him, shouting, "No! NO! Pitter-Patter, I don't know if I can fix this! What have you done?"

But Pitter-Patter hadn't done anything...

I lifted my nose from the ground, stunned, unsure what to do next. Meanwhile, I could tell that Snicker was getting impatient. He tapped his flip-flop at me. I had to act before he dragged me back to the sidewalk. I stalled, pretending that I had to find the perfect spot to pee. Finally, with just the right amount of dramatic flair, I found the spot where I *knew* Pitter-Patter would get my message. I squatted in the grass and left my response: "Pitter-Patter, I will help you prove that you did not leave Hiccup in those old leaves. We'll talk tomorrow at the Baseball Farm."

CHAPTER FOUR

A few days a week Mr. Garcia and The Vacuum meet at the Baseball Farm to throw the ball around and usually Pitter-Patter and I tag along.

The Baseball Farm is a neighborhood park a few blocks from our house. It contains a playground that I am not allowed to go on, for reasons that have never been explained to my satisfaction. There's also a walking trail that loops around it, and several baseball fields. I think it has a boring human name, but it really is a farm for baseballs, so that's what the neighborhood dogs call it. Humans are sometimes not that good at descriptive names.

A dog can go to the Baseball Farm any time and select any baseball they want from the field! I've found some real beauties over the years. The real trophies are retrieved during an actual baseball game, especially if the flavor from the pitcher's glove hasn't worn off. I've always found it unfortunate that the baseball players don't appreciate how fresh and delicious these baseballs are. Haven't they ever tasted one? Instead of expanding their horizons and tasting one for themselves, they usually get all shouty, screaming, "Get off the field!"

Rude.

I woke up the day of my meeting with Pitter-Patter and took a quick pee break outside. I zipped back in the house to check my bowl, just in case a ham fell in there. You never know.

The Bark Park was closed that day for fence repairs so there were no classes, giving me some extra time to practice my invisibility skills. I finished my breakfast and headed towards the living room. A new couch had been delivered earlier that week, and it seemed like the PERFECT place to work on my invisibility. I also needed to prep for my meeting with Pitter-Patter later that day. I assumed my natural Attorney-at-Law instincts would carry me through the meeting, but it couldn't hurt to review the few facts that I had gathered from Pitter-Patter's peemails.

Crunchy sidetracked me with a hug. Curse my huggable-ness! Couldn't she see I had work to do?

I wriggled out of her hug and flicked my nose at her to signal that she was interfering with my work schedule. And then, she said those fateful words that always get my attention: "Do you want a belly rub, my Precious Snoozle-Doozle?"

Ding-dang it! I *had* to resist this delightful offer. I *had* to practice being invisible on the fancy new couch and think about how to help Pitter-Patter!

Instead, I found myself on my side, stretched out from paw to paw… maybe just a quick one? Heavens, I had become so drowsy. Surely I could fit in a power nap before I begin working? I ambled over to my bed on the floor and plopped down. I fell into the perfect snooze.

"Mrs. R., are you ready to go?" The Vacuum jangled my leash, waking me up. He also made a somewhat personal remark about why I hadn't woken myself up with the sound of my own "snoring", which is unlikely, because I only do delicate, precious snores. The Vacuum clipped on my leash, and we made the short walk to the Baseball Farm.

I had accidentally slept through the time I'd set aside to practice my invisibility skills and prep for my meeting with Pitter-Patter but figured it would be okay. There would be other opportunities to practice my invisibility skills, surely. And it's not like I hadn't read Pitter-Patter's peemails—I totally did. I just hadn't given them a lot of additional thought. But part of being an Attorney-at-Law is thinking on your paws. I could totally do this. I couldn't wait to talk to Pitter-Patter and learn more about my first case!

We arrived at the Baseball Farm. The Tiny Tornadoes Tee-Ball team had started their spring training. Suddenly, I heard my favorite song, the cracking sound of a bat connecting to a whiffle ball. I slammed to a halt. The Vacuum stumbled into me. I wish he would be more aware of his surroundings. I started to chase the ball but realized that an Attorney-at-Law would be All Business when talking with a client, so I let it go. I am the Best at Being All Business.

"Hey guys!" Mr. Garcia and Pitter-Patter had arrived. Together we headed over to the wide-open space where dogs can play off-leash. Free of our leashes, Pitter-Patter and I stuck to our routine so as Not to Arouse Suspicion. Not Arousing Suspicion is a very important part of being a dog. Otherwise, it would be impossible to sneak extra treats. Pitter-Patter and I play-bowed at each other, then chased each other in a circle. When I saw that Mr. Garcia and The Vacuum were occupied with their game, I slowed down and whispered to Pitter-Patter.

"Did you get my peemail?"

"I did! I didn't know you were a lawyer! I am so grateful that you are taking my case."

"Yes, well, it's a recent development in my life," I said, with my Trademark Confidence. "How did you get into so much trouble? Why didn't this stay between you and the Garcias?"

"Well," said Pitter-Patter, "we were at the Bark Park, and Mr. Garcia was telling that guy who is *always* there with his Chihuahua about what he thought I'd done. Sneaking Hiccup outside and dumping him in the leaves! I would never do that. I have my own toys. I even have a stuffed pizza slice! Next thing I know, this Chihuahua drops a peemail nearby, telling me that he's some sort of local prosecutor and

is going to press charges under the Intentional Destruction of a Stuffed Animal Law! My court date is in six days at the Bark Park. You've got to help me. If I'm found guilty, I'll be shunned in the neighborhood for a whole week! No one will bark at me, or play with me, or even sniff me! It will be terrible. I'm really scared."

I paused. This was serious. I'd heard of that Chihuahua. His name was Brooks. He finished law school two years ago. A good dog, but a tough prosecutor. My first case and it was going to be a doozy. And technically, I still wasn't a real lawyer. I filed that thought under "details to worry about later," and turned back to Pitter-Patter.

"Alright," I said. "I need to visit the scene of the crime. I'll make sure tonight's walk takes me to your house so I can look for evidence to clear your name. With only six days until your court date, I'll have to move fast."

(I'd have to move very fast. Six days until Pitter-Patter's court date, and six days of law school to go! I was cutting it very close. Thankfully I am the Best at Time Management.)

We were both exhausted after all that chasing. We ambled over to Mr. Garcia and The Vacuum, ready for home. I needed another power nap, stat. Tonight was going to be busy.

CHAPTER FIVE

That night, The Kitchen prepared one of my favorite meals, homemade macaroni and cheese. I can smell cheddar from five hundred meters away. Cheese is another one of my passions, although running in the sprinkler remains my greatest love. Just listen to how it sounds: *Sprinkler.*

When dinner was ready, Snicker set the table, and everyone sat down. I placed my muzzle first on Snicker's leg, then Crunchy's, and gave them the look I reserve for when I am on my best, most adorable cheese-deserving behavior.

Everyone ignored me.

"HMMPH," I thought. Then I realized that The Kitchen's

mac and cheese recipe had probably gone the way of her veggie burger recipe. By ignoring me, Snicker and Crunchy were probably trying to protect me from another of The Kitchen's questionable culinary experiments.

The meal ended and it was time for my walk. Fortunately, Crunchy was on walk duty tonight. I knew it would be easy to convince her to stop and play with Pitter-Patter for a few minutes while I examined the scene of the crime. She clipped on my leash, and we popped down the front steps and walked to the edge of the driveway. I sat and waited for Crunchy to give me the signal. "Let's go!" she commanded and led me down the sidewalk.

Oh no! Pitter-Patter's house was in the opposite direction! I stopped on the sidewalk and angled my head in the other direction, tugging on the leash.

"Toasty Banana Pancakes, what are you doing?" she cooed, trying to coax me along. I tilted my chins up at her. And then me and my adorable chins lay down smack in the middle of the sidewalk. Was I proud of this? No. Did I have to do it? Absolutely.

"Fine!" Crunchy huffed and began walking fast in the direction of Pitter-Patter's house. I felt the tug of my leash and popped right up, trotting along next to her. I started barking as we approached the house, signaling to Pitter-Patter that I was nearby. He barked from inside the house. Mr. Garcia opened the kitchen door and Pitter-Patter bounded out just as we walked past. His timing was perfect. Crunchy spotted him and squealed, "PITTER-PATTER LOOK HOW CUTE YOU ARE TODAY!" (She is so predictable.)

We stopped near the gate. Mr. Garcia greeted us from the doorway.

"Hey guys! Do you have time to stop and say hello?"

"Of course!" replied Crunchy.

Mr. Garcia walked to the gate and opened it. Crunchy and I stepped into the yard. Just as we'd planned at the Baseball Farm, Pitter-Patter picked up a tennis ball. He carried it to Crunchy and dropped it on her toe. She unclipped my leash, reached down, picked up the ball, and threw it for us to chase.

Pitter-Patter dashed after the ball. I started to chase the ball, then cleverly detoured to the back porch where Pitter-Patter had found Hiccup and began sniffing for clues. I am the Best at Clever Detours.

When I got to the pile of leaves where Pitter-Patter had discovered Hiccup, I poked my nose right in there and inhaled a big, giant Attorney-at-Law sniff. Hmmm. I dug my nose in further. What were these scents? Hints of rabbit tickled my nose. A whiff of last summer's spilled lemonade lingered. Oh no! Is that ragweed? I am terribly allergic to ragweed! I sneeze-barked, then continued my sniffing. Was that the tiniest sensation of… me? WHAT? I hadn't done anything! Was I being framed?

Wait, no. I remember sneaking back here for a quick pee during the Garcias' last barbecue. What I did not smell, however, were any odors that indicated that Pitter-Patter had been back here long enough to bury Hiccup in an old leaf pile. There was only a tiny, stale whisper of Pitter-Patter— about as much as I'd expect to sniff for a dog who'd been back here just long enough to retrieve Hiccup. If Pitter-Patter had hidden Hiccup here intentionally, I would've smelled a Pitter-Patter tsunami—there would have been waves of scent everywhere.

This was good news. I had the first bit of proof I could use to clear his name. I dropped my shoulder and rolled onto my back, collecting every speck of evidence. As long as no one tricked me into taking a bath, I'd have all the details with me when we arrived at our court date. And no one tricks Mrs. R. into a bath.

I knew I'd need more than this one small bit of proof. I definitely needed more evidence, and a witness. That would be ideal. But where on earth would I find one?

"Mrs. R.! Puppy-friend, where are you?" Crunchy was calling for me. The sun was setting. I left a fresh peemail for Pitter-Patter, detailing my findings, and trotted back towards Crunchy. "There you are, Snuggle-McFuzzle Biscuits," she said, clipping my leash back on. "Time for us to head home."

She waved good-bye to Mr. Garcia and Pitter-Patter and led me back through the gate and down the sidewalk to our house.

CHAPTER SIX

The next morning, I was bouncing off the furniture, eager to get to my next class at Wagsworth Legal Academy. I also needed to stay on top of my case. The Kitchen is no fan of pets *or* children ricocheting off the furniture, so I knew she'd want to hustle me to the Bark Park a bit earlier than usual. She clipped on my leash and led me to the minivan.

We arrived and I launched myself out of the van the second the door slid open. "Mrs. R.! Heel!" shouted The Kitchen. (When I hear that tone in her voice, I know it's time to put on my Best at Following Instructions face and get my act together.) I joined her and she picked up my leash. As we walked towards the entrance of the Bark Park, I gazed at the portable toilets. I do love reading a good human peemail. They are rarely interesting, but I still like to check.

After we walked through the entrance to the Bark Park, The Kitchen secured the gate and unclipped my leash. I zipped over to Wagsworth Legal Academy and joined my classmates.

"Mrs. R., you're just in time!" barked Dr. P. "Today, you and Maple Lane will work with me as we examine two cases—the Case of the Killer Paw and the Case of the Misguided Photo Bomb."

Darn it. I'd hoped to practice my invisibility skills again with Dr. Shadow. I guess that would have to wait.

"Nice of you to make it," said Maple Lane.

I ignored him. "Good morning, Dr. P.!" I barked.

Maple Lane and I followed Dr. P. to his classroom near the stick pile. I paused to scratch my neck. My allergies were really acting up.

"Are you planning to join us, Mrs. R.?" asked Maple Lane impatiently.

I finished scratching and caught up to Maple Lane and Dr. P., Maple Lane was already hogging the best shady spot under the tree. I settled into a spot in the sun to hear Dr. P.'s lecture. I wish I had sunglasses.

"Today's case study, the Case of the Killer Paw, focuses on an event where at first everyone thought a terrible accident had occurred. Our world is full of accidents—an excited tail wag sends a glass flying off the coffee table, a spirited sprint through the house knocks a plant to the floor, the trash bin tips over when you're trying to retrieve a partially used sandwich… I could go on and on. Most of the time, these accidents are messy for humans to deal with, but harmless. The Case of the Killer Paw is an important case in canine law because this accident… was deadly."

I gasped. Even Maple Lane looked horrified.

My snuggly chins and I leaned forward, eager to learn more.

Dr. P. continued, "It was an early summer evening, in a two-story green house with wood floors. The family had settled onto the couch to watch some TV, while their dogs, a retriever named Clarinet, and a collie named Hurricane, half-dozed on the floor. The entire family noticed a housefly creeping across the floor towards Clarinet, who jolted awake as the fly tiptoed onto her paw. To their surprise, Clarinet gazed lovingly at the fly, and the fly appeared to return her adoring gaze with his many eyes."

"Romance! GROSS," interrupted Maple Lane.

"Please continue, Dr. P.," I said graciously. I am the Best at Being Gracious. Maple Lane rolled his eyes.

"The fly flew from Clarinet's paw and landed on the floor near the coffee table. Clarinet followed, fascinated. Her nose was just inches from the fly. Clarinet's family started teasing her good-naturedly. 'Look who has a new man in her life!' they chuckled. Suddenly, the UNTHINKABLE happened. There was the tiniest squishy SQUELCH as Clarinet's paw touched down on her Fly Guy and then, nothing. The family said teasingly, 'Clarinet! You've killed your fiancé!' They laughed and returned to their TV show. Clarinet lay down sadly beside Hurricane, who'd watched the whole scene from his dog bed on the floor."

"Dr. P., I have a question," I barked. "How did Clarinet end up going to trial?"

"Well Mrs. R., I'm getting to that. Clarinet stayed sad all night. Even Hurricane seemed sad. The pair dragged themselves through what was usually a boisterous morning walk. Finally, when they reached their favorite tree, Clarinet left a long, sad peemail, which began with 'I'm a widow!' and ended with, 'I'm sorry that I squished your guts onto the floor. You're in a better place now, in the trash bin now, among the leftovers. I'll never forget you. Please forgive me.'"

I sniffled. It was my allergies, I swear.

"Later that day, Big Ten walked by and read that peemail. Even though it sounded like an accident, she knew the court needed to investigate Fly Guy's death by squishing. She left a peemail for Clarinet, ordering her to appear at court in two weeks."

Maple Lane interrupted again. He cannot help himself. "I don't understand. This is a clear case of Accidental Squishing. Clarinet feels terrible. Isn't that enough?"

"Actually, Maple Lane," said Dr. P., "the court has an obligation to investigate every insect death by dog, even when the dog swears it was an accident. First, the court must determine that The Squish was in fact accidental. Second, the court needs to understand if the accused canine could have done something that might've prevented The Squish. In this case, the evidence showed that…"

He paused. I barked my I Must Know More! bark. My paw itched and I settled down to give it a few licks. Honestly, these danged allergies!

"The romance between Fly Guy and Clarinet was a fraud. And Hurricane was in on it."

Maple Lane yipped gleefully. "I KNEW IT!"

My head shot up from my paw-licking. "You did not!" I barked back. "Two minutes ago, you said this was a clear case of Accidental Squishing!"

"Students!" growled Dr. P. "Let me finish!"

Maple Lane and I settled down. "Sorry, Dr. P.," said Maple Lane.

"The evidence gathered by the prosecution, along with a confession from Hurricane, revealed that Fly Guy had been bothering Clarinet all day. He landed in her food, on her nose, and buzzed constantly around her ears. Clarinet got madder and madder, until she decided that a Murderous Squish was her only option. But how could she make it look like an accident? She and Hurricane put their heads together and came up with a plan. Humans, they knew, would not be able to resist a fly/dog love story. Between the human witnesses to the 'romance' and the phony 'I'm so sad' peemail, they figured that no one would suspect a thing. Unfortunately for them, Hurricane and Clarinet didn't know that *every* Squish is investigated by the court."

I breathed deeply. Case of the Killer Paw, indeed. I sneezed. Pollen. Ugh.

"What happened to Clarinet and Hurricane after they were found guilty?" I asked.

"Well," said Dr. P., "Clarinet had to write and leave an apology peemail for Fly Guy's 32,765 closest relatives. She also had to turn her favorite toy, a stuffed turkey, over to the court. Finally, she was not allowed to eat any snacks she found on the sidewalk for six months."

"WHOA," I barked.

"What about Hurricane?" asked Maple Lane.

"Because he was in on it, but wasn't the actual Squisher, Hurricane received a lighter sentence of three months of Community Service. Once a week, he had to write a peemail, educating the canine community on the importance of all insects. Each peemail featured a different type of bug—spiders, flies, millipedes—anything with the potential for squishing. The goal was that other dogs would Think Before They Squish."

This time I interrupted. Unlike Maple Lane, I am the Best at Suitable Interruptions. "How did the court know they were guilty?"

"Hurricane confessed to everything," said Dr. P.

"Really! Why?"

"He couldn't take the guilt. His conscience got to him."

"And they went back to living in the same house after all this? How did they do it? Weren't they mad at each other?"

"Mrs. R., I don't have an answer for you. That's between them," replied Dr. P., "And it's important to understand that if you are going to be a successful Attorney-at-Law, it doesn't matter. Your job is to represent your clients. Sometimes those clients *will* be guilty, and they must take responsibility for their actions, including damaged friendships."

I sat quietly. Even Maple Lane paused. Until now, I'd never considered that I might have a guilty client. Dogs are careful observers of humans, and we know they make bad decisions all the time. Honestly, if a human leaves a slice of cheese pizza on a coffee table, they *must* realize that they are inviting a dog to eat it, or at the very least, lick it. This case though… this was the first time I'd learned of a *dog* making a bad decision; actually, it was a lot of bad decisions, starting with the moment that Clarinet began plotting her revenge on the pesky fly. Would I have done the same? What would Maple Lane have done?

WAIT A MINUTE. I couldn't know what Maple Lane would have done. But I darn well know what I would've done. In my distress over this case, I'd nearly forgotten that I am the Best at Resolving Conflicts! PHEW. I would never have turned to an Intentional Squish. I would've invited a pestering fly to a BuzzBark event, where we could've gotten to know each other and learned what we had in common, like a shared dream of finding the lid open on the kitchen trash bin.

Dr. P. interrupted my thoughts with a question. "Mrs. R., Maple Lane, do you have any more questions about the Case of the Killer Paw?"

"Nope!" we barked.

"Then let us continue with our study of the next case, the Case of the Misguided Photo Bomb."

CHAPTER SEVEN

I stood to attention. This case didn't sound the least bit familiar. I leaned in, listening closely.

"Like the Case of the Killer Paw, this case involves two dogs living in the same home," said Dr. P. "Their names were Howard and Austin. Howard was three years older than Austin and he had a bit of a reputation around the house. Howard was an adventurous eater and was always on the lookout for a new snack, even if it was still on the stove! Howard loved being a solo act, so when he arrived home one day to find Austin, he was not impressed."

Maple Lane broke in. "That's how I'd feel if Mrs. R. showed up at my door. Not impressed."

I glared at Maple Lane. "Can you repeat that, Maple *Avenue*?" I asked. "I couldn't hear what you said over the sound of your terrible attitude."

"Students!" barked Dr. P. "Knock it off!"

He returned to the details of the case. "For two years, Howard tolerated Austin. He wasn't mean, but he wasn't exactly friendly. Sometimes he'd trick Austin into eating something that is really bad for dogs. For example, one time Howard encouraged Austin to eat a whole bunch of chocolate candy that was wrapped in foil. Chocolate can be very dangerous for dogs, as you know. Fortunately, Austin has an iron stomach and could eat just about anything, so he was okay. However, when he went out into the yard to use the bathroom, things got… sparkly, from the tin foil."

Maple Lane laughed.

"It's not funny!" I barked. I never joke about sparkles.

"Dr. P., did Howard face any charges for that? It sounds like he broke a whole pile of laws with that prank."

"No, Howard didn't face charges," said Dr. P. "Austin believed it was an accident and forgave Howard right away. Not long after that, though, Howard went too far."

Maple Lane and I both leaned closer. "Tell us!" barked Maple Lane.

"It was family picture day," began Dr. P. "Howard and Austin, being part of the family, were scrubbed and brushed until their fur shined. They even had new, matching collars. The photographer arrived and began arranging the humans into their spots for the family picture. After the humans were in their places, the photographer called for Howard and Austin and had them sit in front. Howard and Austin sat very still and looked right at the camera. The photographer began snapping away. It took some time for the humans to relax. In the first photos, their eyes were often closed, or someone was sneezing or picking their nose."

I interrupted. "Humans are *gross*."

"I agree!" barked Maple Lane.

Dr. P. gave us both a look and cleared his throat. "May I continue?"

We nodded.

"No one paid attention to Howard and Austin, who continued sitting very still. Finally, the humans relaxed, and when Howard sensed everyone smiling the perfect smile, he made his move. He lifted his leg..."

I gasped.

"...and left a peemail on Austin right as the photographer snapped the photo."

"ULTIMATE photo bomb!" said Maple Lane.

"Dr. P., what happened next?" I asked. I had to know.

"At first, nothing happened. Remember, the humans weren't paying much attention to Howard and Austin. It was only later, when they were reviewing the photos, that they discovered that the one picture that had all the humans smiling, also featured Howard peeing on Austin's leg. As you can imagine, the humans spread this story far and wide. They thought it was hilarious—and maybe to humans it was. But in the dog world, it was a direct violation of Peemail Code 0723A: No Dog Shall Engage in Peemail for the Entertainment of Humans. Peemail is our main method of communication, and it *must* be taken seriously! We can't be leaving junk peemails all over town, and on each other, no less! It's a terrible waste of messaging resources."

I nodded in agreement.

"So, what happened to Howard?" asked Maple Lane.

"Well, there was a mountain of evidence against him. His family had shared the picture with everyone, including the humans at the home where Brooks lived. There was no question of Howard's guilt. When faced with the evidence, he pleaded guilty immediately, rather than trying his luck in the courtroom."

"What was his sentence?" I asked.

Dr. P. drew a deep breath and began to tremble. "Here's where it gets really bad. Because this happened at the end of October, right around Halloween, Howard was sentenced to..."

"Just say it!" yelped Maple Lane.

"Wearing any costume his humans chose and being on his best behavior the *entire time* it was on."

We sat in silence as the horror set in.

"I feel sick," said Maple Lane.

"Do you know what the costume was?" I asked.

"It was... a cat costume," said Dr. P.

I glanced at Maple Lane. He was turning green. I felt queasy myself. Just then, I heard my name.

"Mrs. R. Let's go!" called The Kitchen.

"Thanks Dr. P., for a great class. You've given us a lot to think about," I barked.

As I ran across the Bark Park towards The Kitchen, I thought about my client, Pitter-Patter. The stakes were high. What if I messed up and Pitter-Patter was found guilty? What if his punishment was the same one that Howard faced? I'd never forgive myself. I had to get my act together. So far, all I had was his word and a bit of scent, or really, a lack of scent from a leaf pile in his backyard.

The Kitchen clipped on my leash and we jogged back to the minivan. By the time the door slid open, I promised myself that I would spend every extra minute searching for evidence to clear Pitter-Patter. He was a Good Dog. Now I just needed to gather more evidence to prove it. Aaaaaannnnnnndddd graduate from Wagsworth Legal Academy before Pitter-Patter's court date. But that was a minor detail. I am the Best at Not Getting Bogged Down in Minor Details.

CHAPTER EIGHT

My next walk rolled around and it was The Kitchen's turn to accompany me. I pressed my nose to the sidewalk the instant we left the driveway, eager to collect more evidence to prove Pitter-Patter's innocence. I veered from the sidewalk to check out a huge collection of unread peemails. News of squirrel sightings, a dropped hamburger, and gently used tennis balls made it nearly impossible for me to focus.

"HEEL!" commanded The Kitchen.

I came back to her side and we continued down the sidewalk. We arrived at the corner, and spotted Popsicle and his person ambling down the sidewalk. I barked "Hello!" and

Popsicle returned my greeting. The Kitchen and I stopped and waited for Popsicle and his person to catch up so we could walk together.

"Mrs. R.! How've you been?" asked Popsicle.

"I'm doing alright. Did you hear I'm at Wagsworth Legal Academy now?"

"Yes! What's it like?"

We ambled along and I told Popsicle about Wagsworth Legal Academy and Maple Lane.

"You're going to be a terrific lawyer, Mrs. R. Don't let Maple Lane get to you."

"Thanks Pop," I responded. "What's new with you?"

"Well, you heard about that PB & J I had, right?"

I nodded.

"So that didn't end so well. I was in and out of the house for hours, with a lot of... emergency bathroom breaks. After that, my person said I couldn't have any more street food—all I could have was 'dog' food. Now it's the same boring thing, two times a day. No surprise flavors, no interesting textures... it's just crunch, crunch, crunch. BLECH."

"I'm sorry to hear that, Popsicle. I wish I could help you."

"You can!" Popsicle barked slyly. "Keep your nose on high-alert for a little 'sidewalk special'. It's trash day—maybe someone dropped something when they put their trash bins at the end of the driveway. If we find something, you create a distraction and I'll gobble it up. Pleeeeeaaaassseee," he begged.

I put on my almost-a-lawyer hat and considered his request. Would I break any laws if I helped out my friend? No. This seemed on the up-and-up.

"It would be an honor," I replied.

I am the Best at Helping a Hungry Friend.

Popsicle and I tuned our noses to high alert as we continued walking, our people chattering away behind us. Suddenly, Popsicle and I both pulled hard to the right, catching our people by surprise.

"MRS. R.!" shouted The Kitchen. I ignored her and dragged her with me towards the source of the magnificent smell. She stumbled in the grass and clung to my leash as I dashed towards the aroma.

It was a FISH! In the grass! I could hardly believe it!

We live close to the river and a pair of bald eagles nest nearby. Eagles swoop onto the river and catch the fish. I'd heard rumors that sometimes a fish slipped from their talons and landed in our neighborhood, but I'd never seen one before. The canine world is full of urban legends just like this fish tale—The Cheese that Got Away and The Great Sidewalk Ham. And now, here I was, on the brink of having a fine dining experience I had only dreamed about: Grassy Old Fish. I drooled as I pulled The Kitchen closer to my prize.

"My arm!" yelled The Kitchen. "Mrs. R. Snugglesworth! Heel! HEEL!"

Popsicle barked frantically, "Mrs. R.! Remember our deal? You're the distraction! I get the snack! It's mine!" He

plowed forward as his person furiously tried to tug him back to the sidewalk.

My desire to eat that glorious fish made me forget all about the deal I'd made with Popsicle moments earlier. My inner furry rhinoceros stampeded towards that fish and snatched it right up. I rolled it around my jaws, savoring the grimy deliciousness. It was an amazing mix of grass and fish, with just the right amount of dirt sprinkled in. *Heavenly.* Popsicle tried to snatch the fish from me, but I dashed down the sidewalk, fish firmly between my teeth.

Popsicle's person yanked HARD on his leash. "Popsicle! No! No! Let's go! Sorry, guys, but I've got to get him out of here."

I lay down on the sidewalk with my find, and watched Popsicle get dragged home in the opposite direction. That's a shame. I wonder what he did?

The Kitchen approached me quietly, worried that I'd run away. She leaned down gently and picked up the end of my leash.

"Mrs. R.! Release! Release!"

I gave The Kitchen one of *my* Signature Looks. A look that said, "*Fine dining cannot be rushed.*"

My jaws remained clamped for a few more seconds around my treasure which was quickly turning into a pile of fish guts. I chewed what remained of the fish and swallowed it.

The Kitchen checked her watch. "Shoot! Look at the time! We better get home."

She turned me around and we headed back to the house. I could NOT WAIT until it was time for me to write my next set of peemails. The story I would tell! I'd need to choose my words carefully. Grimy. Exquisite. Masterpiece. Sensational! I am the Best at Writing Reviews of Fine Dining.

After all that excitement, I settled into deep-snooze mode, briefly snapping to attention only when I heard the refrigerator open. Even when I'm worn out, my snack instincts stay sharp. When I finally awoke, I was surprised to see that morning had arrived and was thrilled to discover I still had a hint of fish breath. I heard Snicker calling for me. It felt a bit later than usual.

"Mrs. R.! How about a walk?"

Still tired, I trundled to the front door where he was waiting for me. I yawned while he clipped on my leash. I took my position at the edge of the driveway. "Let's go!" he shouted, and off we went. The fresh air woke me up. I picked up my pace as we neared the oak tree. I was eager to leave an announcement about my gourmet sidewalk fish.

I set my nose to the "super-sniffer" setting as we approached the oak tree. Before I told everyone my fish news, I wanted to catch up on my peemails. Hmmm. I had a message from Pitter-Patter. I sniffed more closely.

"Hey Mrs. R.! Thanks again for taking my case. I can't wait to hear about the other evidence that you turned up. You're going to do great in court."

What was that about? Oh no. No! No! No! I had forgotten all about Pitter-Patter's case! AND slept right through the time we usually went to the Bark Park! I missed my class today! What was I going to do? I left a short message for Pitter-Patter.

"Everything is under control. I am totally ready for your case. See you at court in three days!"

Everything was not under control. We only had one bit of so-so evidence. Also, I was getting into the habit of lying to my client, which I suspected would be frowned upon by the professors at Wagsworth Legal Academy. I decided that for the next three days, every minute that wasn't spent napping, snacking, avoiding baths, or attending law school would be spent scouring the neighborhood for evidence to clear Pitter-Patter. Surely I would find something.

CHAPTER NINE

My plans to devote my attention to my law classes and Pitter-Patter hit a huge roadblock, called non-stop rain. For the next three days, it did nothing but rain. And rain. My walks were quick zips around the block, with no time to sniff for evidence. Going to the Bark Park was out of the question. This is why I love the sprinklers but despise rain. Rain ruins plans. Classes at Wagsworth Legal Academy were cancelled automatically whenever it rained, so instead of attending classes and searching for evidence, I paced the house constantly, stopping only for naps and snacks. A few times each day, The Vacuum said, "Mrs. R., you are going to wear a path into the floor!"

With each step, I felt the weight of my worries. My legal career was going to come to a crashing halt before it started. And Pitter-Patter! Would he ever forgive me?

After three days and nights of rain, the skies finally cleared, just in time for Pitter-Patter's court date. My family was eager to get back into our routine of breakfast, then Bark Park. After three days of pacing, I'd decided to go to Pitter-Patter and recommend that we ask the judge to move his court date to next week. That way, I'd have enough time to finish my classes and find some more evidence—and Pitter-Patter would never have to know about my screw-ups… you know, the whole napping away my time after I caught my fish and the whole not-really-being-a-lawyer situation. THIS is why I am the Best at Creating Flawless Plans.

The Kitchen interrupted my thoughts. "Car ride!" she shouted.

Snicker clipped my leash onto my collar and we headed down the porch steps and towards the minivan. The door slid open.

"Up!" he commanded.

I leapt in and headed to the backseat. "You're so good at riding in the car!" cooed Crunchy.

My family is always telling me that I am The Best at Riding in the Minivan. This is one hundred percent true, even on long trips. There's one thing about car rides that I find a tiny bit disturbing, though. When I get in the minivan and look up, there's always a very fun, well-behaved, and I suspect brilliantly smart dog staring back at me from a tiny reflective window in the middle of the front seat. I cannot lie, she seems enchanting. And yet… we have never managed to meet in person. The second I get out of the car, she disappears. I don't know what that's about.

We arrived at the Bark Park. I paced nervously in the minivan. "Hold on Mrs. R.!" said The Vacuum. "I wonder why she's so anxious? She must really need some exercise after being stuck inside for three days."

He slid open the door and reached for my leash. I jumped down and tried to shake out my nerves. Pitter-Patter had placed his fate in my paws, and there was a good chance I was going to let him down terribly. The rest of the family clambered out of the car, and we set off down the path to the Bark Park.

CHAPTER TEN

There were a bazillion peemails on the trail into the Bark Park.

We walked past the soccer fields and the portable toilets. I was too worried to even try to read the human peemails. They were probably very boring anyway.

We continued through the field and finally reached the gate. Crunchy lifted the latch and we entered the Bark Park. I spotted Pitter-Patter and my tail wagged nervously. I took a deep, practically-an-Attorney-at-Law-but-technically-not-one breath and headed towards him.

"Pitter-Patter!" I barked. "Good to see you, old friend. Listen, with all of the rain, I didn't get to search for more evidence to clear your name. Let's go to the judge and ask if we can postpone your court date."

"Why?" asked Pitter-Patter. "You left me that peemail telling me that everything was under control."

Oh boy. I felt TERRIBLE. I'd been lying to Pitter-Patter from the beginning. It was time for the truth. "Walk with me," I said.

We trotted off to the far corner of the Bark Park. "I have a confession. I'm technically not a lawyer... yet. I'm taking classes at Wagsworth Legal Academy and figured I'd be done by the time your court date got here."

Pitter-Patter just stared at me, and then he did something he'd never done before. He growled.

"There's more." I barked nervously. "When I told you in my peemail everything was fine... I lied. Instead of searching for more evidence to clear your name, I got distracted by a fish I found on my walk."

Pitter-Patter stopped growling. "Wait! You actually saw a fish ON THE GROUND? Was it dropped by an eagle? Where was it? What did it taste like?"

"Pitter-Patter!" I barked. "I'll tell you about it later. Right now, I need you to listen. After I ate that delicious fish, I slept for *ages* and then it rained for the next three days and I couldn't get out much. The only evidence I have is the bit I found in your yard a few days ago. I am so, so sorry. I'm not a lawyer and I have no real evidence to help you anyway. You were counting on me, and I let you down. I was going to tell you another lie about why I couldn't defend you today, but I just… I just… let's go talk to the judge. I'll explain everything."

Pitter-Patter glared at me. "Mrs. R.," he said, "I am really angry with you. Big Ten is the judge assigned to my case. We can ask her for a delay, but I don't know whether she'll agree to it. She is a stickler for staying on schedule. As I see it, we have three problems: 1) You're not a lawyer yet, 2) Even if you were a lawyer, you don't have strong evidence, and 3) YOU DIDN'T SAVE ME ANY FISH."

I gave a sad, solitary bark. The problem with being the Best at Being the Best is that includes being the best at things like Being Distracted by a Fish and Letting Down a Client. (I think we can agree that even though I was technically not a lawyer, Pitter-Patter was still my client.) And, worst of all, Letting Down a Friend.

We trudged slowly to the area of the Bark Park where court was held. My tail drooped as we passed Wagsworth Legal Academy. Dr. Shadow and Dr. P. and all the other Legal Beagles were going to be so disappointed in me. And Maple Lane! No doubt he'd be thrilled by my failure. I felt, as Crunchy would put it, "Like the saddest Bellybutton-Sprinkle-Winkle in the whole wide world."

I sneezed. Even in my most difficult hour, I couldn't escape from my ding-dang allergies. My neck was so itchy! I stopped to scratch. Pitter-Patter stopped too and waited patiently. He is such a good soul! Suddenly, we heard a ferocious bark—not completely unusual—we are at a park full of dogs, after all. But this bark was personal. I looked up to see Popsicle coming straight towards me and Pitter-Patter. What on earth?

Pitter-Patter barked, "Popsicle! Calm down! What's wrong? It's okay, buddy—what could possibly have you so upset?"

Popsicle said, "This isn't about you, Pitter-Patter. This is about what Mrs. R. did to me a few days ago."

I sneezed again and sat back on the ground, mystified. I am the Best at Being Mystified When I Have No Idea What is Going On. "Popsicle, I don't understand. Everything was fine on our walk a few days ago. You were a little grouchy because you weren't allowed to have street snacks anymore, but…" My voice trailed off. I remembered the street-snack deal I'd made with Popsicle on our walk, minutes before we saw that fish. And I remembered how excited he'd been by my promise to help him out… the promise I broke the second I got a whiff of that delectable, magical, silver-scaled, perfectly aged fish. My tail drooped in shame.

"But what, Mrs. R.?" Popsicle barked. "I'm sure you told Pitter-Patter about the fish you found. Did you tell him the whole story? Did you tell him how moments earlier you'd promised to distract our owners if we spotted a street snack, so I could have it? Did you tell Pitter-Patter how good old Popsicle had been eating nothing but DOG FOOD for two days?"

Pitter-Patter gasped. "Mrs. R.! No!"

My tail drooped even lower. "I'm sorry, Popsicle."

"I'm sure you probably are, Mrs. R.," he replied, "but that doesn't change what you did. Now it's just day after day of boring old DOG FOOD. No fun. No flavor sensations or grimy textures. All I have are memories—like that PB & J I found. Tough at the back end, but totally worth it."

"I'm really sorry, Popsicle. That was a rotten thing to do. I just saw that fish and I got carried away. I didn't think about you at all and I broke my promise. Lately I've been the Best at Lying and Breaking Promises—I was rotten to Pitter-Patter too. I let him believe I was already a lawyer and could take his case, even though I was still in law school. I had good intentions, but the fish was so exciting and I was so tired… and then it rained for three days… Anyway, those are just excuses. I messed up, big-time. We are on our way to see Big Ten right now, to see if she will postpone Pitter-Patter's case so he can get a proper lawyer. We need to prove that Pitter-Patter didn't steal Hiccup from Mr. Garcia. And Pitter-Patter deserves a lawyer who can make that happen."

"Hold on, Mrs. R.," said Popsicle. "I think I may be able to help you and Pitter-Patter."

I leaned into Popsicle and sniffed carefully. I smelled… Hope. Truth. Victory. Redemption. After all, I am the Best at Turning Things Around.

CHAPTER ELEVEN

I was feeling better for the first time in days. There was, however, the tiny issue of Pitter-Patter's case starting in a half hour. And the teeny-tiny issue where I hadn't exactly finished law school yet.

I gulped and glanced over at Wagsworth Legal Academy. Maple Lane was barking the ears off of the Legal Beagles and Dr. Shadow, probably bragging about how great he was. Knowing him, he was saying how he didn't even need to finish the classes, he could just skip right to the exam. What a… why was I thinking about him right now? Wait. Wait. WAIT. I thought back to the first day of class. *To obtain a law degree, you have two options: 1) Prove your knowledge of* *all three examples of case law **and** invisibility, or 2) Prove your invisibility skills **and** jump the bar.*

Option two was a possibility! If I could demonstrate my invisibility expertise and jump the bar, I'd get my degree in time to represent Pitter-Patter! Technically I hadn't yet made myself invisible, but I was so close the last time—I could do it! And honestly, am I not The Best at Not Worrying About Technicalities? I'd gotten this far, after all. But the bar. THE BAR! That thing was almost as tall as me—that's why I was so good at going *under* it. The *only* thing that's tricky about being seventy-pounds-of-low-to-the-ground PRECIOUS is gravity—it really interferes with my jumping.

I took a deep breath. "Pitter-Patter, I am going to get my degree and be ready for your case in thirty minutes. I PROMISE. Popsicle, thank you for your offer to help us out. Be ready to take the stand." And with that, I left Pitter-Patter and Popsicle and ran as fast as I could to Wagsworth Legal Academy.

I barreled into Wagsworth Legal Academy and slammed to a stop when I reached Dr. Shadow, who had a fresh haircut and smelled like a medium-rare sirloin steak with a hint of sweet potato. No doubt he came to class straight from a patient visit. When this was all over, I was definitely going to ask him about my allergies.

"It's the furry rhinoceros!" shouted Maple Lane. "I figured you'd given up."

I ignored him. "Dr. Shadow, I would like to take my exams right now. Is that possible?"

"I think so," he replied. "But let me double-check with Dr. P."

Dr. Shadow scampered over to Dr. P. They exchanged a few muffled barks. Dr. Shadow returned to where I was waiting with Maple Lane.

"Dr. P. and I agree, Mrs. R.," he said. "You can take your exams. But why so soon? You haven't finished all of the classes, so your only option is to demonstrate your invisibility skills and jump the bar."

"I know," I sighed. "I didn't plan for it to be this way, but my mouth got ahead of my plans, and I need to be a real live Attorney-at-Law in twenty-eight minutes."

Maple Lane had been listening the whole time. He was literally drooling. UGH. "Hey Mrs. R., you can hire ME as your lawyer when you get charged with FRAUD. I'll even give you a discount! As soon as you finish messing this up, I'm going to do exactly what you're doing, only I'm going to pass with flying colors! I've been jumping that bar since I was a pup, and you KNOW I can turn invisible."

I grimaced. "Maple Lane, I don't have time for your comments right now."

Then I turned to Dr. Shadow. "I know that I messed up, believe me. But I'm going to try to make it right. Right now."

Dr. Shadow, Dr. P., and the rest of the Legal Beagles gathered near the edge of Wagsworth Legal Academy, where they would have a clear view of the picnic table where I was to prove my invisibility skills. Maple Lane and the other students stood behind them, eagerly waiting to see what happened.

"Mrs. R. Snugglesworth," barked Dr. P. "You are trying to pass your law school exam without completing your training. This is highly unusual and very risky. You have chosen to prove you are ready to become an Attorney-at-Law by demonstrating your invisibility skills and by jumping the bar. You will begin with your invisibility skills. There are three parts.

1. You must get on top of the picnic table.
2. You must become invisible.
3. A human must remark on how good you are at being invisible, and then walk away.

Are you ready?"

I gulped. "Yes, Dr. P.!" I barked.

I approached the empty picnic table. It would be easy to jump up there, but I might have to stay invisible for a long time until a human came along. I jumped onto one of the bench seats, and looked around. Still no humans nearby. I jumped onto the table itself. YES! I had completed part one. I settled onto my stomach and closed my eyes. I envisioned my water bowl, and the stillness of the water inside it. I concentrated harder and heard the soft twist of a lid being removed from a fresh jar of peanut butter. I focused my thoughts and heard the barest whisper of a spoon scooping up a dollop of peanut butter... my breathing slowed... and there it was. Invisibility.

I heard a murmur of approval from Dr. Shadow and the Legal Beagles. Now came the hardest part. I needed a human

66

to confirm my invisibility, and fast. Another thirteen minutes had passed, leaving me with only fifteen minutes before I was due in court. I heard footsteps coming closer, followed by a human voice with a hint of know-it-all-ness. Of COURSE. The human was Maple Lane's person. He must be coming to pick up Maple Lane. He spotted me and strode to the picnic table. I could smell the lunch he had tucked into his backpack—egg salad sandwiches. Gross. Double-gross. I'd eat one of The Kitchen's veggie burgers before I'd eat an egg salad sandwich. Must. Suppress. Gag. Reflex.

"Off!" he said.

I ignored him.

"Down!" he said.

I continued to ignore him, laying as still as I possibly could. How could he even see me? I was invisible!

"Move!" he said.

I ignored him and inhaled the tiniest breath… and released the tiniest, most precious delicate snore you can imagine. A butterfly could not have snored more gently.

I heard a sharp bark from the direction of my classmates. Maple Lane! What was he doing?

His owner turned towards him, and, walking away from the picnic table, called out, "Hey Maple Lane! Looks like this dog on the picnic table is the Best at Being Invisible. Even better than you!"

Inside my head, my tail wagged gleefully, while I continued to lay stock-still in a move I call "Extra Credit."

Dr. Shadow scampered over and barked, "Congratulations Mrs. R.! That was a magnificent example of invisibility. You have passed the first part of the exam. Now it's time to jump the bar. We better hurry—your case starts in… ten minutes! Let's get over there!"

CHAPTER TWELVE

I leapt down from the picnic table and followed Dr. Shadow to the bar. This was going to be interesting. And terrifying. Ten minutes from now, I'd be representing my first client in court… or be down a couple of friends AND be looking at the end of my legal career.

My classmates had joined the professors near the bar. Maple Lane barked, "You got lucky on the invisibility, Mrs. R.! Better hope your luck lasts because we all know you STINK at jumping over the bar."

"Maple Lane, I will speak to you after class!" growled Dr. P. "You need a refresher on professional behavior. Perhaps you're not cut out to be a lawyer, with an attitude like that. Stop wasting our time!"

Was it me, or did Maple Lane look ashamed? It was about time.

Dr. P. resumed his regular bark. "Alright, let's do this. Mrs. R., you have three tries to make it over the bar. Are you ready?"

"Yes!" I lied.

I ran back a few paces so I'd have room for a running start. I paused and looked at the bar. It was set to the highest height, approximately eighteen inches off the ground. I gave a determined bark and charged forward. I got close to the bar… and jogged around it. My classmates groaned. Maple Lane, still stung by his talking-to from Dr. P., managed to keep his comments to himself.

I sneezed. Dang it! Two more tries and just over eight minutes until my court case. I rushed back to the starting line and took off at top speed. This time, I leapt as I approached the bar. My front legs catapulted over the top. I stretched as far as I could, but I felt the metal of the bar graze my back legs. The bar wiggled, then clanked to the ground. NO. This is the worst possible thing that could happen.

It's embarrassing to admit, given how smart dogs are, but we need a human to put the bar back on its stand. I was down to seven minutes, and the humans were yards away, chatting about human peemails, probably. It was over. I hung my head and laid down. Pitter-Patter would hate me now. Just then, I heard a flurry of know-it-all barks. GREAT. Maple Lane was seizing the opportunity to torment me. A few seconds later, I got a whiff of egg salad sandwiches. Oh yuck—not this again. This was going from terrible to ultra-terrible. But wait... wait... the sound of footsteps reached me seconds after the egg salad stench. I looked up. It was Maple Lane's person!

"Looks like the bar fell down," his person remarked, bending down and lifting it back into place.

I stood up and looked at Maple Lane as his person walked away. "Thanks," I barked.

Maple Lane looked at me. Did I detect a glimmer of respect in his eyes? "Don't stand there thanking me," he said. "You've got one more try and your case starts in six minutes! Get back there and try again!"

He was right. I sprinted back to the starting line and gave the bar a final look. There was a lot riding on this. If I made this jump, I could represent Pitter-Patter in court and

hope that one day he'd forgive me. Popsicle might forgive me, too—maybe he'd even be proud of me! My reputation as the Best at Completing Law School Using Unique Methods would become legendary.

I began my sprint towards the bar, furry-rhinoceros style. My bundle of adorable chins flapped against my chest. As I neared the bar, I jumped, stretching my front half forward as hard as I could. I felt my low-to-the-ground-precious belly graze the top of the bar, and then felt my back paws touch the ground. The bar wiggled… jiggled… and STAYED IN PLACE! Yes! I did it! I passed the bar! I was an official Attorney-at-Law! And my case started in three minutes.

"Well done, Mrs. R.!" barked Dr. P., as my classmates cheered joyously. "You better hustle to the courtroom! You've hardly any time to spare!"

She was right, of course. I turned my head, nodded at Maple Lane, and ran to the courtroom. It was time to get some justice for Pitter-Patter.

CHAPTER THIRTEEN

I spotted Pitter-Patter pacing nervously in front of grove of trees that marked the entrance to the courtroom. "Pitter-Patter! I'm here, I'm a lawyer for real! Let's do this."

"Oh, thank goodness," he replied. "I'll get Popsicle. He's by the trash bin, sniffing around and remembering a happier snack time."

"Popsicle!" he barked. "Pop! Mrs. R. is a real lawyer. Hurry! We've only got one minute before my trial starts!"

"Popsicle," I said. "I really appreciate you taking the stand. Remember that you're not doing it for me—you're doing it for Pitter-Patter. You can stay mad at me for as long as it takes—I know I deserve it. But Pitter-Patter… you know what a good soul he is. Thank you for helping me get him out of this mess."

"You mean the mess you made?" he retorted, and then paused. "Alright. I'll do it. Just remember—you and I still have a few things to resolve. I'm doing this for Pitter-Patter."

Popsicle hustled over and the three of us entered the courtroom. Brooks, the prosecutor, nodded curtly in our direction. I returned his nod with an Attorney-at-Law nod of my own. I am the Best at Attorney-at-Law Nods.

"Cutting it rather close, aren't you, Pitter-Patter?" asked the judge, Big Ten. She turned her tiny self towards me. "Mrs. R.! I see you took my advice and enrolled in Wagsworth Legal Academy. It's amazing that you qualified as an Attorney-at-Law so quickly."

"Well, Judge," I said modestly, "It turns out that I—" Popsicle bumped me, interrupting my speech. How rude. Apparently, Popsicle had forgotten that I am the Best at Graciously Accepting Compliments.

Big Ten called the session to order. Pitter-Patter and Popsicle sat down next to each other. I gave a quick shake to get rid of my nervous energy. It was go time.

As the prosecutor, Brooks spoke first. He turned to the jury.

"Canines of the jury, today we are gathered to hear the charges against Pitter-Patter, for Intentional Destruction of a Stuffed Animal. In this case, the stuffed animal is a forty-year-old stuffed rabbit named Hiccup. Hiccup began his life with Mr. Garcia, when Mr. Garcia was just a small boy living on the other side of the world.

"As Mr. Garcia grew older, Hiccup retired from daily use, but he was still always part of Mr. Garcia's life. When Mr. Garcia moved across the ocean, Hiccup came along. And when Mr. Garcia made his yearly trips home, Hiccup was always carefully tucked in his luggage, just in case. Hiccup held a special place in the heart of every member of the Garcia family. When he wasn't traveling, he rested in a tidy drawer, where he wore a tiny red-and-tan knitted sweater."

"I object!" I barked.

"To what, exactly?" asked Big Ten.

"The color of Hiccup's sweater is irrelevant to the facts of the case."

"Your Honor," said Brooks, "It's important that the jury know the color of Hiccup's sweater. Those are his best colors! The fact that Mr. Garcia took the time to knit Hiccup a sweater, in flattering colors, helps show how important Hiccup was to Mr. Garcia."

"Objection denied!" declared Big Ten. "And Mrs. R., use your objections wisely."

"Yes, Your Honor," I replied.

Brooks continued his speech. "Pitter-Patter was caught *with Hiccup in his mouth.* As you know, this is a serious charge. We all have our own toys already. Stealing a beloved family stuffed animal, particularly one as important as Hiccup, cannot be tolerated. Imagine that someone in your family took your favorite stuffed animal and did something awful to it. Imagine they—I can barely say it—took your favorite stuffed toy and WASHED it. Our canine community simply cannot allow behavior like Pitter-Patter's to go unpunished. When one dog steals a human's stuffed animal, it hurts all of our reputations."

He sat down. I rose from my spot on the ground and gave the jury my best Attorney-at-Law bark. I didn't have a whole lot as far as evidence went—but I was determined to present it with flair, confidence, *and* pizzazz. (You will not be surprised to learn that I am the Best at Pizzazz.)

"Members of the jury, fellow canines, I, Mrs. R. Snugglesworth, Attorney-at-Law, am here to represent our dear friend and neighbor, Pitter-Patter, who has been falsely accused of harming a beloved family stuffed animal. I will present evidence *and* a witness who will demonstrate, without a doubt, that Pitter-Patter DID NOT take Hiccup and leave him in the bushes.

"On the day in question, Pitter-Patter was doing some important business around the back deck at his home. To his surprise, he found a tiny stuffed bunny named Hiccup, damp, grubby, and scrunched up next to the deck, under some dead leaves.

"Alarmed, Pitter-Patter unearthed Hiccup with his paw and gently picked him up and brought him to the back door to his person, Mr. Garcia. He carefully set Hiccup on the ground in front of Mr. Garcia. Instead of the you-rescued-my-beloved-stuffed-animal ear-scratch he anticipated, he heard only disappointment in Mr. Garcia's voice: 'Oh Pitter-Patter. What have you done?'

"Friends, jurors, can you imagine how Pitter-Patter felt in that moment? He had just *rescued* Hiccup and instead of being rewarded for his good deed, he was *accused* of *stealing Hiccup.*"

The jury sat riveted, except for four or five dogs that wandered off. Fortunately, some new dogs barreled over and after some meet-and-greet sniffs, the case continued.

"My client," I continued, "found Hiccup in the bushes. I will now prove to you that my client is innocent of the charges against him. I give you," I paused dramatically, "Exhibit A."

I thrust my neck at the jury. They looked confused. I moved closer. "Sniff my neck!" I barked. "I visited the scene of the alleged crime, rolled in the crime scene, and gathered the evidence myself. Do you smell an intense mix of Pitter-Patter and the odor of a well-traveled, elderly stuffed rabbit wearing an adorable knit sweater? No. NO YOU DO NOT. I challenge you to pick up any scent other than the faintest whisper of Pitter-Patter and Hiccup. You can't, can you? And why is that? Why, you ask?

"It's because Pitter-Patter didn't put Hiccup in the bushes. He didn't steal him from inside the house somewhere and bring him to the bushes at the back of the deck. No! Pitter-Patter was outside when he *spotted* poor Hiccup in the bushes, and he rushed over to *rescue* him. At that exact moment, Mr. Garcia spotted Hiccup, and leapt to the wrong conclusion." I returned to where Pitter-Patter and Popsicle sat and paced dramatically.

"I object!" barked Brooks. "How does the jury know that you didn't tamper with the evidence? You could've..." he paused. "*Bathed*."

I stared at Brooks in disbelief. Yes, technically I had practiced law without being a lawyer for a few minutes... okay, days... and so I suppose one might argue that I get creative with the rules. I expected him to dispute my evidence—even *I* knew my evidence wasn't that good— but to accuse me of *bathing*? That was low. Was he intimidated by my obvious gifts for lawyering?

A hush fell over the jury. And then they started barking like crazy. Bathed? Bathed! The scandal! The judge began barking. "Order! Order in the court! Brooks, what's going on?"

I interrupted before Brooks could respond, using my Best at Being the Best Attorney-at-Law bark. "Judge, please. Obviously, I would never, ever, in a million years take a bath. Do I love the sprinkler? Of course. Everyone knows that. Drinking fountains? Magical. But a bath? With soap? Never."

The judge nodded. "Jurors, please ignore what Brooks said. Mrs. R., is your witness ready?"

"Yes, Your Honor," I barked. "I call Popsicle to the stand."

CHAPTER FOURTEEN

I waited. The jury looked around. A few of them fought over a chewed-up frisbee.

"Ahem. Popsicle."

"Here I am!" Popsicle rushed over from Pitter-Patter's side.

"Popsicle," I began, "I'd like you to take us through the events on the day that Pitter-Patter supposedly stole Hiccup and left him in a pile of old leaves."

"Okay. I actually need to start by telling you the night before."

"I object!" barked Brooks. "How could Popsicle's activities the night before the crime have anything to do with this case?"

"Your Honor," I said. "Please allow me to proceed. I promise that what Popsicle did the night before is important and establishes *why* he witnessed what he saw the next day."

"I'll allow it," said Big Ten.

Brooks glared at me. I ignored him.

"What happened the night before?" I asked.

"Well," said Popsicle, "As you know, I live near the elementary school and in nice weather the kids eat lunch outside. I was out for my usual walk on Sunday evening. As we walked past the school, my spectacular sniffer led me to a peanut-butter-and-jelly sandwich that only had a few bites taken from it! My person wasn't looking, so I gobbled it up in one giant gulp. At that moment, it tasted DELICIOUS. Just the right amount of peanut butter. It had rained over the weekend, so the bread wasn't too dry. Sometimes a snack just comes together. It was my lucky day!"

Brooks interrupted. "Judge, where is Popsicle going with this story? This has nothing to do with the case!"

Big Ten said, "Mrs. R., have your witness get to the point, please."

"Okay, Popsicle," I said. "We've established that you found a slightly used peanut-butter-and-jelly on the ground. Now, please tell us how this relates to Hiccup."

"Well, here's the thing," admitted Popsicle. "It wasn't a lucky find. Because the next day..."

"Yes?" I prodded. "What happened the next day?"

"The next day my stomach didn't feel too good. I didn't

want to eat anything and I really had to go to the bathroom. A lot. In fact, after a few close calls on the living room carpet, my person took me for a walk once an hour, just to be on the safe side. It was on one of those trips that I saw Mr. Garcia carry a basket of wet laundry outside. He hung everything up on the clothesline, including Hiccup."

"Aha!" I barked. "So, what you are telling us is that you saw *Mr. Garcia* take Hiccup outside, not Pitter-Patter?"

"That's exactly what happened," said Popsicle.

I turned to the jury. "Jurors," I barked, "Popsicle's testimony confirms Pitter-Patter's innocence. It's quite obvious that Hiccup slipped from the clothesline during his air-dry and fell into the pile of leaves. I ask that you find my client not guilty and clear him of all charges."

Big Ten spoke: "Brooks, do you have a response?"

"No, Your Honor," he barked. His tail drooped with disappointment. He knew it was over.

Big Ten sent the jurors off to make their decision.

CHAPTER FIFTEEN

I paced nervously, even though I was feeling pretty confident. Popsicle really came through for us! Moments later, the jury delivered the verdict to Big Ten: Not Guilty!

"Pitter-Patter," said the judge, "You are free to go."

"You did it, Mrs. R.! Thanks for taking my case," barked Pitter-Patter.

"Anytime, Pitter-Patter," I said. "Thanks for sticking with me, even after I messed up. We got lucky—without Popsicle's testimony, we might have been in trouble. Popsicle, I hope you can forgive me someday."

"Just give me some time," he barked gruffly. "I'll get there."

I wagged my tail. The next time I saw a good street snack, I'd hide it and leave a peemail for Popsicle so he'd know where to find it. He and I were going to be okay. Maple Lane ran over to me. "Not too bad, Mrs. ARGHHH," he barked. "Who knows? Maybe someday I'll hire you to help me out of a jam." He sprinted away before I could respond. I thought about what he said. Was Maple Lane just making conversation, or was he in some kind of trouble?

Snicker shouted, "Mrs. R., let's go!" I sprinted over to my family. After all, I am the Best at Following Instructions.

"What did you get up to, my Precious Toodly-Doodly?" asked Crunchy. "Did you have fun playing with your puppy friends?"

Playing? Playing! My first case, and she thought we were playing? Humans can be clueless. The Kitchen clipped my leash onto my collar. As we opened the gate to leave the Bark Park, I left a quick peemail on the fence with my business card. After all, where better to advertise my services than at the courthouse?

We arrived at the minivan. The Vacuum slid the door open. "Up!" he commanded, and I jumped in. "You're the BEST at jumping into the car," cooed Crunchy.

EPILOGUE

As the car backed out of the parking lot, I reflected on the events of the day. Did I win my first case? Yes. Did I make some mistakes? Yes. About a katrillion of them. On the plus side, when next time gets here, I'll already be a lawyer. Bonus! I wonder if they'll miss me at Wagsworth Legal Academy. Probably. And it wouldn't be so bad to go back and finish up those other classes and maybe find out what Maple Lane was talking about when he said he might need me as a lawyer. I hope he's not in trouble. I'll ask him the next time I bump into him. He certainly came through for me today. Wait. Are we friends now?

I am the Best at Giving Second Chances.

We pulled into the driveway. The Vacuum slid the door of the van open. "Down!" he commanded.

I hopped down and we all went inside. Snicker unclipped my leash. I was exhausted. That case really took it out of me. I ambled over to my bed and plopped down, my eyes already half-closed. I fell into a delicious nap, where I dreamed about a yard with two sprinklers and a full-time hot-dog stand. I am the Best at Dreaming Perfect Dreams.

The End.

ACKNOWLEDGMENTS

To quote Mrs. R., I am the Best at Saying Thank You. (I hope!)

When I announced I was writing a book about a dog who becomes a lawyer, and by the way, her name was Mrs. R. Snugglesworth, lots of people burst out laughing, in a good way—just the reaction I was looking for.

Thank you to my friends and family who shared their own stories, feedback, and counsel: Renee, Maggie, Lucy and Nick Canavos, Carrie Casper, Elizabeth Flanagan, Suzanna, Margot, and Gwyneth Flanagan, Angelica Giraldo, Lucinda Metzger, Maddie and Sophia Moore, Rachel Orr, Don Sandberg, Karen Sandberg, Mary Sandberg-Reed, Jennifer Scott, Wendy Simms, Leonard Thompson, and Cedric Wright.

A special thank you to Lisa Davis, who shared her editing expertise and made this story infinitely stronger. Truly a pleasure.

To my husband Gene, thank you for calling our lovely yellow lab, Tenzing, a "Mrs. Snugglesworth" one extra snuggly morning. To my daughter, Riley, thank you for insisting she was actually "Mrs. R. Snugglesworth" and announcing she was your lawyer. To my son, Chase, thank you for listening to my daydreams, plans, and ideas on our Wednesday nights. This story is my love letter to all of you.

And finally, to Tenzing. Thank you for understanding when we call you Mrs. R.

CPSIA information can be obtained
at www.ICGtesting.com
Printed in the USA
JSHW030440210622
27294JS00006B/213

9 781915 036094